COLONY HIGH BRANCH LIBRARY

D0531983

SUMMER

AN ALPHABET ACROSTIC

ONTARIO CITY LIBRARY
AUG - - 2005
ONTARIO, CA 91764

SUMMER

AN ALPHABET ACROSTIC

by Steven Schnur
Illustrated by Leslie Evans

CLARION BOOKS
New York

Clarion Books
a Houghton Mifflin Company imprint
215 Park Avenue South, New York, NY 10003
Text copyright © 2001 by Steven Schnur
Illustrations copyright © 2001 by Leslie Evans

The illustrations were executed in hand-colored linoleum blocks.
The type was set in 19-point Galliard.
Art direction and book design by Carol Goldenberg.

All rights reserved.

For information about permission to reproduce selections from this book,
write to Permissions, Houghton Mifflin Company, 215 Park Avenue South, New York, NY 10003.

www.houghtonmifflinbooks.com

Printed in Singapore

Library of Congress Cataloging-in-Publication Data
Schnur, Steven.
Summer: an alphabet acrostic / by Steven Schnur ; illustrated by Leslie Evans.
p.   cm.
A companion volume to Autumn: an alphabet acrostic and Spring: an alphabet acrostic.
ISBN 0-618-02372-0
1. Summer—Juvenile literature. 2. Acrostics—Juvenile literature. [1. Summer. 2. Acrostics. 3. Alphabet.]
I. Evans, Leslie. II. Title.
QB637.6 .S36   2001
793.73—dc21   00-031674

TWP   10 9 8 7 6 5 4 3 2 1

For Grandma Eva,
whose warmth embodies this season

—S. S.

To my grandmothers:
Margaret Warden Mays, whom I knew and loved,
and Mary Lewis Evans, whom I wish I had known

—L. E.

Above the nursery
Window, shading the
Newborn baby asleep
In her crib and a
Nest of robins, a
Gleaming striped canopy.

Blankets and umbrellas,
Endless miles of sand,
And the
Constant
Hum of wind and waves.

Close by
A glittering
Blue lake, high
In the mountains,
Nestles a fishing lodge.

Dragonflies dart
And hover,
 Inspecting white flowers with
Sunlike
Yellow centers.

Everyone is already up
Attending to chores when the
Rooster crows, these
Longest days of the
Year.

Fourth of July banners wave from
Lampposts, front porches,
And the village
Grandstand as the parade
Streams by.

Green clusters, soon to be
Red
And
Purple,
Entwine the
Stairs.

Heavy boots, a canteen,
Insect repellent, and a
Knapsack full of food for our
Early morning walk.

In the July heat we
Doze in hammocks and
Lie on the
Emerald grass.

Jumping
Over
Gray stone walls and
Gullies,
Enjoying an early
Run.

Kelp and foam float by
Each sailboat racing
Eagerly to the finish
Line.

Large ships head
Into port,
Guided safely
Home by tall
Towers perched
High
On cliffs, their
Unceasing beacons
Sweeping the coast
Each night.

Millions
Of tiny
Stinging insects
Quick to strike
Unsuspecting victims
In the
Twilight
Of mid-
Summer.

Noisy crickets, the
Incandescent
Glow of fireflies, and flashes of
Heat lightning fill
The dark garden.

O ver hill and dale,
R ipening apples,
C herries reddening,
H ives swarming with bees,
A nd long
R ows of
D angling pears.

Paper plates and cups,
Iced tea and lemonade,
Chicken salad sandwiches,
Nuts and chips, watermelon,
Ice cream and soda,
Chocolate cake and blueberry pie.

Quickly slipping
Under the fence at the
Abandoned
Rock pit, the
Rowdy children leap
Yelling into the cold water.

Rocks and pebbles hurled
Into still
Pools form
Perfect circles that grow
Larger and larger, then
Echo off the shore.

Tumbling waves
Inch up the beach,
Depositing seaweed and shells, then
Ebb slowly away.

Upright in the
Moist sand of the nearly empty
Beach, keeping the sun's
Rays out of our
Eyes this
Last
Lazy weekend
At the shore.

Vines of cucumbers,
Ears of corn,
Gourds,
Eggplants,
Tomatoes,
Acorn squash,
Beans,
Lettuce, and
Endive,
Slowly ripening.

Waiting
Outside in neat stacks
On the porch for the first chilly
Day or night.

XII weeks with not
Even an inch of
Rain have ended
In a
Crackling thunderstorm.

Yawls
And sailboats,
Cutters and sloops, are
Hauled out of
The water as summer ends.

Zigzag lines
Of stars
Divide the heavens
Into
Autumn's twinkling
Constellations.